The Elves and the Shoemaker

Retold by Rob Lloyd Jones

Illustrated by John Joven

Once, there was a famous shoemaker. Lords and ladies loved his beautiful boots, and even kings wore his slippers.

But now the shoemaker was old. He had aches and pains from sewing and stitching.

No one wanted to buy his shoes or his boots anymore. All day long his shop sat silent and empty.

The shoemaker stared at his last piece of leather, and sighed.
"After this, I don't know what we will do."

"Let's worry about it in the morning," his wife said, as she led him away with a hug.

But morning came with a big surprise. There on the workbench sat a fantastic pair of brand new shoes.

Everyone admired
the shoes in the window.
They were sleek and shiny
and perfectly stitched.

What fine
footwear!

The shoemaker sold
them the moment he
opened his shop.

The next morning came with an even bigger surprise.
Two pairs of boots stood on the shoemaker's bench! And what
incredible boots they were, with twirly patterns and golden toes.

The shoemaker sold them in seconds. "Oh my," said a customer. "Never have I seen such elegant boots."

"Heavens," gasped another. "Just look at those laces and handsome high heels."

The strange shoe magic continued for weeks. Every morning, when the shoemaker woke, there on his workbench were more fabulous shoes.

Each day they were finer than the last.

They had **Shiny** buckles...

twirly ribbons...

...and **pretty** bows tied
in leather and lace.

Word spread: the shoemaker is back to his best!
People came from far and wide
to buy his splendid shoes.

But the shoemaker felt strange about this change of fortune. He knew that his shoes were not really *his* shoes at all.

"Let's hide in the workshop tonight," he said to his wife. "We'll see who is making all these wonderful new shoes."

That night, the shoe shop door opened with a quiet creak.

Two shadows flitted through the silvery moonlight,
and soft feet padded across the floor.

Two tiny creatures in raggedy clothes sprang onto the workbench.
They were giggling and grinning and dancing and singing.

"Elves?" thought the shoemaker.

Smiling and singing, the elves set to work, hammering heels, stitching leather and making fluffy pom-poms.

By the first light of morning, the latest pair of shoes was finished, and the cheery little elves scampered away.

The shoemaker gasped
and his wife clasped her hands.
"What magical creatures!"
she cried.

"We must repay their
kindness," the shoemaker
said. "But what can
I make for an *elf*?"

For the first time in weeks, the shoemaker sat at his workbench, cutting and stitching leather and cloth.

He worked and worked, as day became night. His candle burned down and his eyes ached in its flickering light.

Finally he was finished. He left what he had made for the elves to find.

"Those creatures have given us so many wonderful surprises,"
he told his wife. "Tonight they'll have a surprise of their own."

The elves squealed with joy when they saw the shoemaker's gift. "What stunning new suits," they said in delight. "Such terrific top hats and tails."

The elves danced all around the workbench,
gleefully singing about their magnificent suits.

What happy little elves are we,
no longer workmen shall we be.

We look so fine in our new suits, no longer shall we stitch new boots.

The shoemaker and his wife watched the happy elves
skip off into the night.

Thanks to the kind little creatures, they could live
comfortably for the rest of their lives.

The shoemaker never made
another pair of shoes. But
whenever he thought of
the elves, he smiled.

He hoped they were
still singing and dancing
somewhere, in their fine
hand-stitched suits.

About the story

The Elves and the Shoemaker was first written down by brothers Jacob and Wilhelm Grimm. The Grimm brothers, who lived in Germany around 200 years ago, loved fairy tales. They collected lots of other stories too, including *Cinderella* and *Snow White*.

Edited by Lesley Sims
Designed by Laura Nelson

First published in 2016 by Usborne Publishing Ltd., Usborne House, 83-85 Saffron Hill,
London EC1N 8RT, England. www.usborne.com Copyright © 2016 Usborne Publishing Ltd.